This book belongs
to

_____

EZRA JACK KEATS

PET SHOW!

THE MACMILLAN COMPANY, NEW YORK, NEW YORK

ISBN: 0-590-75760-1

Everyone was talking about the pet show.

The kids told each other
about the pets they would bring.
Matt said he would bring ants!
"I'm gonna bring my mouse!" bragged Roberto.
"What are you gonna bring, Archie—the cat?"
"Uh-huh," said Archie.

The next day they all got ready for the pet show.
"Where's the cat?" Archie called.
"Anyone see the cat?"
Archie and Willie looked in the cat's
favorite hangouts, while Peter and Susie
searched up and down the street.
No cat.

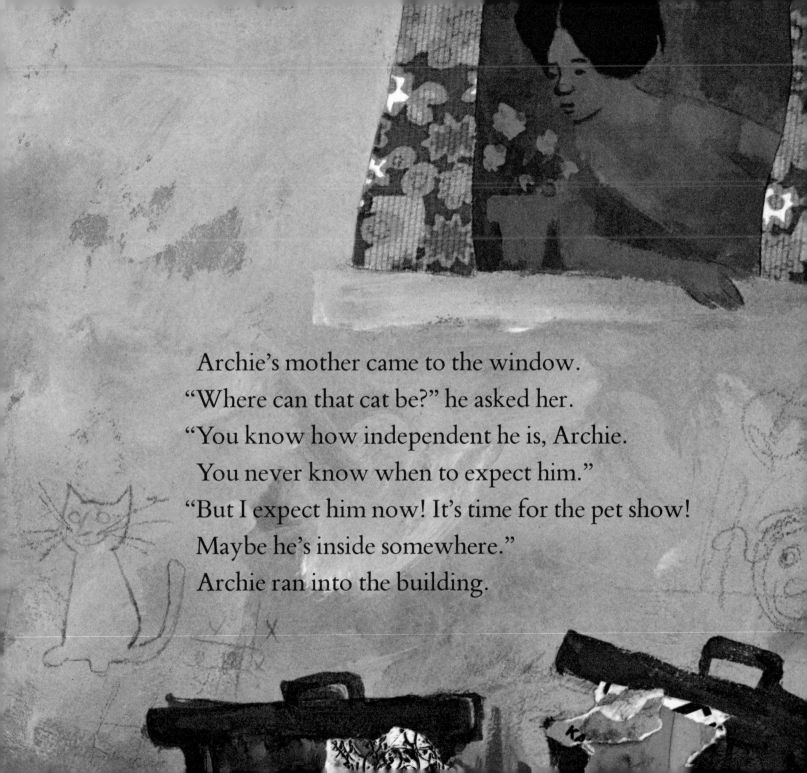

Archie's mother came to the window.
"Where can that cat be?" he asked her.
"You know how independent he is, Archie.
You never know when to expect him."
"But I expect him now! It's time for the pet show!
Maybe he's inside somewhere."
Archie ran into the building.

After a while he came to the window.
"I can't find him. I looked all over the place.
   You'd better start without me."
"Gee, we're sorry, Archie," said Peter.
"So long," said Susie.

They got to the entrance.
A lot of people were already there.
Just then Roberto's mouse took off.

Willie chased the mouse.
Roberto chased Willie.
Peter chased Roberto.
Susie chased Peter—
and the show started.

"Line up with your pets, please!"
the judges called.
They walked up and down, looking carefully
at every pet, and asking, "How old is your pet?"
and "What's your pet's name?"

Everyone got a prize for something.
There was the noisiest parrot,
the handsomest frog, the friendliest fishes,
the yellowest canary, the busiest ants,

the brightest goldfish, the longest dog,
the fastest mouse, the softest puppy,
the slowest turtle—
and many more!

As the last prize was awarded,
someone shouted,
"Look–here comes Archie!"

"Hello. You're just in time!" a judge said.
"What's in that bag?"
"My pet."
"May I see it, please?"
   At that moment the cat showed up.

The other judge called out, "A blue ribbon to the nice lady for the cat with the longest whiskers!"

Before anyone could say anything, he pinned
a blue ribbon on the old woman and came back to Archie.

"What kind of a pet have you got in that jar?"
"A germ!" answered Archie.
"Mmmm—and what's your germ's name?"
 Archie thought for a moment.
"Al," he said.

The judges whispered to each other.

"A blue ribbon for Al, the quietest pet in the show!" the judges announced.

As everyone was leaving,
the old woman came over to Archie.
"He's really your cat, isn't he?" she said.
"You should have the ribbon."
"It's OK," Archie said. "You keep it."
And he ran to join his friends.

They passed the old woman on their way home.

"Thank you for the ribbon," she called.

Archie smiled.

"It looks good on you. See you around."

"See you around," she said.

The Children's Choice® Clubhouse

It's the perfect place for playing or for curling up with a good book ★ Big enough to hold a few friends (it's 3′ x 4½′ and 4½′ tall) ★ Made of sturdy corrugated cardboard with a washable finish ★ Decorated inside and out with whimsical illustrations in full color ★ A very special gift.

To order, please send your name and address with a check or money order for $19.95 to:

**Children's Choice® Clubhouse
Scholastic Inc.
900 Sylvan Ave.
Englewood Cliffs
New Jersey 07632**